Other adventures in this series:

Five Go Gluten Free
Five Go Parenting
Five Go on a Strategy Away Day
Five on Brexit Island
Five Give Up the Booze
Five Forget Mother's Day
Five Lose Dad in the Garden Centre
Five Get Beach Body Ready
Five Get on the Property Ladder
Five at the Office Christmas Party
Five Get Gran Online
Five Go Bump in the Night
Five Escape Brexit Island

FIVE GO
ABSOLUTELY
NOWHERE

Enid Blyton®

FIVE GO
ABSOLUTELY
NOWHERE

Text by
Bruno Vincent

Enid Blyton for Grown-Ups

Quercus

First published in Great Britain in 2020 by

Quercus Editions Ltd
Carmelite House
50 Victoria Embankment
London EC4Y 0DZ

An Hachette UK company

A CIP catalogue record for this book is available
from the British Library

ISBN 978 1 52941 208 6
Ebook ISBN 978 1 52941 210 9

Text by Bruno Vincent
Original illustrations by Eileen A. Soper
Cover illustration by Ruth Palmer

10 9 8 7 6

Typeset by CC Book Production
Printed and bound in Great Britain by Clays Ltd, Elcograf S.p.A.

MIX
Paper from
responsible sources
FSC® C104740

Papers used by Quercus are from well-managed forests and other responsible sources.

Contents

A Game of Shadows   1

Lockdown Blues   8

Exercising Rights   20

Elder Care   30

The Wild Hunt   39

Hunter S. Gatherer   49

Time Lords   60

The Julian Calendar   66

G.O.A.T.   74

On the Beach   82

Lockdown Life   85

Mine! All Mine!   90

Love Island   97

CHAPTER ONE

A Game of Shadows

A full moon hung heavy in the Dorset night sky. Beneath it, Kirrin Island lay gleaming.

All was still.

At first glance, that is.

Between the castle's crumbling battlements, a masked figure moved with extreme caution, tiptoeing forward, one stealthy foot after the other . . .

Suddenly, a cone of light pierced the shadow, pinning the creeping figure, who covered his eyes and leapt back.

'You've blinded me!' he shouted. 'I thought you said that thing didn't work?'

'Sorry,' said Dick. 'I was just sort of fiddling with it, and it came on.'

'I can't see anything now,' complained Julian.

'Oh – I've got this – it's *Jane Eyre*!' came Anne's voice, from within a tent. 'Is it the bit where Rochester gets blinded?'

1

'It's not part of his charade; it was an accident,' said Dick. 'I put the batteries back in the torch the wrong way round and it came on.'

'I *literally* cannot *see!*' Julian squealed. 'You've burnt my retinas!'

'Besides, I did *Jane Eyre* earlier,' said Anne. 'It would be cheating to do that again. Maybe it's Gloucester from *King Lear*?'

'Or Pacino in *Scent of a Woman*?' George asked.

'Oh, yes, good one,' said Anne.

'It's *not* part of the game!' Julian protested. He stood with his hands on his hips, still unable to see, staring grumpily at where he thought the others probably were.

'Good,' said George. 'Stupid effeminate title anyway, *Scent of a Woman*. Makes it sound like her guffs smell of perfume.'

'Thank you, George,' Anne said. 'How pleasant.'

'I don't know why we have to play bloody charades,' said Julian. 'We aren't a hundred years old.'

'It's because you finally got us kicked off our last quiz on Zoom,' said Anne, 'for arguing with the quizmaster. *Again.*'

'I don't see how it can be my fault,' Julian explained,

'Lockdown will only be a week. Maybe two. We'll be sipping cider in the pub in no time, mark my words!'

still facing in the wrong direction, 'that that oaf didn't know the difference between Yasujirō Ozu and Kenji Mizoguchi! I mean, call that a film round?'

'Oh, shut up,' said Anne.

'And you won't let us play Cards Against Humanity,' Dick said, 'because you refuse to explain to Anne the definition of the word b—'

'No!' said Julian, clutching his ears. 'I'd almost succeeded in forgetting. If only I could scrub it from my brain! Don't say it. *Please*, I cannot imagine Anne knowing that word!' He backed away from them, hands pressed tightly over his ears, singing, 'La la la, I'm not listening to you,' and disappeared into the shadows of the castle ramparts.

'Whose turn is it next?' asked George.

'George!' said Anne. 'There's a dangerous drop over there! He could fall and crack his head!'

'Might knock some sense into him,' said Dick.

They pondered this for a moment before deciding that, on balance, they ought to make sure Julian was okay.

They all scrambled out of their sleeping bags, calling to him. But they now found that they, too, were temporarily blinded by the torchlight.

'Always guessing *Jane Eyre*,' they heard Julian

muttering in the darkness. 'With the facemask on, I thought *Phantom of the Opera* was pretty easy, although I would have accepted *Burglar Bi—* AAARGH!'

'Julian!' screamed Anne. She snatched the torch out of Dick's hand and ran towards Julian's voice. After all the perils they had overcome on this island, to be killed in a stupid game like this would be a terribly ignominious way to go. Even if it did rather reflect their transformation from heroic children to mundane adults.

'*There* you are,' Anne said, as she came round a corner. 'You had me worried then. What are you doing?'

'I backed into a wooden post and got a splinter in my arse,' said Julian, peering round his side, his pyjama bottoms partially lowered. 'I'm trying to get it out.'

'Well, there you're on your own. I don't love you *that* much.' She handed him the torch. 'Come back to the tents. It's nearly eight o'clock. Bedtime.'

'I'm *freezing*,' muttered Julian. 'Glorious sunshine in the day, arctic at night. All my outside bits have practically frozen off.'

'How lovely,' said Anne.

'You're not dead, then?' asked George, as her two cousins came back into the part of the castle ruins where they'd pitched their tents. The torchlight was still predominantly pointed towards the interior of Julian's cotton PJ bottoms, casting disturbing shadows.

'Eight p.m., did you say?' said Julian, looking up into the night sky. 'Might as well be midnight. Isn't there something I was supposed to do at eight?'

Julian nearly jumped out of his skin and dropped the torch as his three compadres rose to their feet in unison, clapping and whooping. Timmy joined in, howling and barking. In the face of this madness, Julian cowered, staring at them.

'Wha–what are you—?'

His hand fell on a device behind him and, turning, he saw that it was his laptop, which had long been left to sleep, carefully propped on a stone shelf. As he touched it, the screen came alive and he saw the light winking beside the webcam.

'Julian!' said a tinny voice. 'Glad to have you with us. Okay, I think that's everyone? Sorry to ask for an evening conference call, ladies and gents, but it was the only time we could all make . . .'

That was what he had been supposed to remember!

Julian was confronted by a checkerboard of pixelated

squares, each showing the looming face of one of his many loathed colleagues, smiling out from their bright and healthy households, like a gallery of judgement.

They couldn't see him like this. Why was this happening? His brother, sister and cousin all clapping and screaming in the background, and him dressed in his PJs!

He leapt forward to slam down the lid of the laptop, but failed to make proper contact, and unthinkingly let go of his pyjama bottoms.

'No!' he screamed. 'Nooooo!'

'Woof!' agreed Timmy. 'Woooof!'

CHAPTER TWO

Lockdown Blues

Reader, they were in lockdown.

A few days earlier, the five old friends-in-adventure (three siblings, one beloved cousin, one extra-beloved dog) had come to stay on Kirrin Island one final time.

It was a chance to reminisce and spend a little time together before life took them on their separate journeys. Anne was moving in with her best friends, Olivia the book publisher and Camilla the doctor (two distinguished professionals who Julian insisted on referring to as 'the saucy vixens'); Dick had accepted a place to study for an M.A. at a Scottish university, starting in the autumn; George was due to leave in the summer to take up a job in San Francisco; and Timmy, of course, would go with her.

Only Julian was going to be left behind, and that was partly why Anne had suggested they come for one last expedition to this old haunt of theirs.

They had arrived on a chilly March afternoon, with a

'We're stuck playing charades, Julian, because you got
us kicked off all those pub quizzes on Zoom!'

view to staying for two nights. Then came the announce-
ment: everyone in the country was expected to stay where
they were. For the foreseeable future.

Here was a group of youngsters (although, with Julian
pushing forty ... but they were still young at heart) who
had always been unashamedly earnest and adamant about
doing the right thing. When it came to an emergency, or a
disaster, or a crisis, they were in their element. But now
they were being told (in so many words, in a direct order
from the prime minister himself) that their country called
upon them to ... to ...

'To just sit on our arses?' asked Julian, turning the radio
off with a snap.

The others, who had been sitting around the campfire to
eat, nodded glumly. They had suddenly lost their appetites.

'But ...' he said.

They looked at him.

'But ...' he repeated. His mind recoiled from this.

'But we can't!' he said. 'We can't just do *nothing*!'

'We have to,' said Dick. 'That is our job.'

It was so unexpected, and counter-intuitive, that
it seemed on the face of it as hard as any task they'd
ever faced.

'We have to go home to London,' he said.

'Why?' asked Anne. 'To be cooped up in a flat? We'll go bananas!'

'We're probably going to go bananas either way,' said George. 'Might as well do it here, where we've got so many happy memories. And fresh air.'

'That's all very well,' said Dick, snapping open a can of Staropramen, 'but, really, we'll have to work from home. We'll need electricity, and broadband and all that . . .'

He tailed off. Each of the four Kirrins was caught up in their own troubles, or at least in the calculation of how many parts of their life had suddenly become off-limits. Pubs and restaurants. Cinema and theatre. Rock-climbing, book browsing, clothes shopping, cricket nets!

'As for electricity and broadband,' said George, 'I might be able to help. You guys remember Raoul?'

There was a sudden cessation of movement round the camp. Furtive glances were exchanged. Whether George noticed or not, she went straight on: 'That boyfriend I had last summer. The reason I couldn't come and see you all for three months.'

'It . . . rings a bell,' said Dick, guardedly.

'Well, he didn't exist,' said George.

11

Julian was about to mouth 'No shit', but Anne silenced him with a frown.

'He was a code word. You see, I knew I had to save up several grand in order to go on this training course last autumn. That meant not coming to London to hang out with you lot every weekend, and I didn't want to get guilted into spending what I didn't have, or borrowing money, or any of that sort of rubbish. In fact, the only way I could make it work was if I paid no rent and worked remotely. So I did.'

'Good for you,' said Anne. 'I'm really impressed!'

'I could never do that,' Julian said quietly. 'You're amazing.'

'I've never loved you more,' Dick said. 'But what do you mean? Where did you live, on a bench in the park?'

'I worked *from here*,' said George, and, so saying, flipped a switch that had been cunningly concealed within the stonework of the castle wall. Elegant soft backlighting suddenly decorated the castle interior.

This was greeted by a most gratifying (to George) chorus of amazement, which redoubled in volume when she popped open a decrepit wooden door to reveal a perfectly insulated cupboard. Inside glowed and winked a cosy-looking bank of server lights.

'Oh Julian, did you get furloughed after all?' Anne asked.
'That's such beastly luck!'

There were also multiple 240-volt plug sockets, a projector, laminated Wi-Fi code, and mini fridge.

'Meet Raoul!' she said.

'George,' said Julian, through the round of applause that followed, 'I'm lost in wonder at your brilliance. Once again.' And, grabbing her round the shoulders, he gave her a big, affectionate smacker on the left eyebrow.

'I am pretty brilliant, it's true,' she said. 'And if you ever kiss me again, I'll break your kneecaps.'

'Woof!' agreed Timmy.

'Hey,' said Dick. 'Dinner's up.'

Anne had dressed and tossed a salad, which was pronounced delicious by all. Dick handed round some paper plates and offered a box of drumsticks, some cheese, pickles and some cold new potatoes.

'Condiments of the house,' he said, offering mayonnaise and mustard.

'What's this?' asked Julian, holding up a slice of brown meat.

'Ox tongue,' said Anne. 'From Waitrose. It was on special offer.'

'Well, lah-di-*dah*,' said Julian, lowering the slice into his upturned mouth, crane-wise.

'Posh a-holes,' said George.

'*Don't* eat it like that,' said Anne. 'It's disgusting.'

'There's a pork pie round here somewhere,' said Dick, 'if anyone wants that.'

'I think this is quite enough. For me, at any event,' said Anne. She knew she was pinching her mouth, despite trying hard not to. I'm turning into my mother, she thought. Please don't let that happen. But then, despite herself: look at that *awful pig* Julian (who had discovered the pork pie crushed against the grass beneath one buttock). Pie as well as ox tongue, as well as chicken. I'd be too ashamed.

To distract herself, she asked Dick where the other supplies were.

'In, as our French friends like to call it,' said Dick, '*le shop.*'

She smiled humourlessly and asked again.

Rather than reply, he nabbed half a pork pie from Julian's plate.

'Oi, you git! I had my eye on that,' said Julian.

'Well?' said Anne.

Julian burped, and everyone made a face, and then

George burped louder and Dick and Julian laughed. Anne, waiting patiently for the tedious boisterousness to subside, came to an awful realization.

'There aren't any other supplies, are there?' she asked. 'Dick? Dick! Will you all please *stop effing burping*!'

The horseplay was suddenly forgotten.

'Come again?' Dick asked.

Anne, after telling Dick that he was fast transforming

'Julian briefly staggered from the pain that shot across his shoulders, down his back, up his legs and buttocks, thanks to Joe Wicks.'

from her beloved sensitive brother into a boring middle-aged toad, explained her concern that there was no more food.

'No,' said Dick, carelessly. 'But there's a boat, and there's a shop.'

'There is also, Dick, my dearest heart, a lockdown,' Anne said.

'Yeah, it's a pain. I'll go in the morning.'

'Where?' she asked.

'Co-op,' he said.

'*Which* Co-op?' she asked again.

'. . . Dorchester?' he said. He shrugged.

'We have no way of knowing if it will be open,' Anne said. 'Nor if we're even allowed to go. What if the car runs out of petrol, and the petrol stations are closed?'

'She's right,' said Julian. 'We can't just go romping through the countryside, looking for a nice farmhouse shop to sell us fresh cream.'

'There will be *rules*,' Anne said. 'And we don't break those.'

Dick looked at Anne with severe disapproval, as though (being the bearer of the news) it was she who had suddenly fabricated this crisis out of fresh air.

'I just don't understand,' said Anne, 'why you've handed out practically all the food we had left, for one meal . . .'

'We won't starve,' said George. 'We're on an island full of . . . well, plants. And rabbits.'

'Woof!' said Timmy.

'They call them bunnies, round here,' said Anne. ('Woof!' said Timmy.)

'And they *are* round here,' said Julian. 'I've seen one, in particular, several times.' (*'Woof!'* agreed Timmy.)

'We've still got breakfast cereal left,' said Dick.

'Breakfast cereal,' said Anne.

'Better than nothing,' said Dick.

'No milk, though,' muttered Julian. 'Finished that with our tea.'

'Actually, now I think about it,' Dick said, 'I'm pretty sure the cereal was in the bag I left on the car roof—'

He broke off, as he saw Anne staring into the fire.

How will we manage life in lockdown, George wondered, without tearing each other's heads off?

'You know, the diet of the future is plant based, and the sooner we get used to that, the better,' said Julian, startling everybody. 'This island must abound in leaves and berries and roots and such that is freely available – and, you know, healthy and vegan, or whatever. It's about time we adapted to it. And I, for one, relish the prospect!'

Julian said this as he lay propped on one elbow, nibbling a chicken drumstick, his mouth and nose shiny in the firelight, from grease; a posture that suggested a Tudor earl at the tail end of a three-day banquet.

Easy for *him* to say they wouldn't starve, the others thought. He'd take a month longer than anyone else.

'After all,' he added, 'lockdown will only be two weeks. Maybe three. Over in no time. We'll be sipping cider, eating cocktail sausages and crammed into the saloon bar of the Admiral Nelson before you know what's hit you.'

'Woof,' said Timmy, his head on his paws, looking into the fire, and thinking about bunnies.

CHAPTER THREE

Exercising Rights

'Up! Up! Up!' shouted George.

'Yes! And stretch! And stretch!' said Anne.

Julian's mind was still piecing itself back together from sleep-dispersed fragments as he peered, blinking, from his sleeping bag. But the sight of his younger sister in figure-hugging Lycra was alarming enough to shock him into full consciousness.

'Wh . . . What are you doing? It's not even ten a.m.!'

'Best part of the day—'

'Oh, don't give me that horseshit. You're turning into Mother!'

'Yeah, give it a rest, Anne,' said Dick, sleepily. 'We've been *asked by the government* to stay at home and do bugger all. Why ruin it?'

'It's started already,' Anne said.

'What has?' Dick asked.

'The crime wave,' said Anne. 'Now we're trapped here,

it's beginning. The whole of Dorset's supply of hand sanitizer, desperately needed throughout the county, was stolen during the night. Ten giant crates of it – swiped from a depot in Boscombe.'

'Swiped!' Julian leapt up. 'You can't be serious.'

'I can. Not a trace left, and no clue as to where the thieves went. No doubt it's on the black web or the dark market or whatever, as we speak!' Anne had the fixed, wide-eyed stare she wore when she encountered injustice.

'Anne,' Dick said quietly, 'we can't do anything.'

She looked to Julian, who shrugged. 'The rules is the rules. We don't break 'em, like you said. We stay here.'

'But this case has got our names *all over it*,' Anne protested.

'Welcome to the lockdown,' said Dick. 'Sorry, Anne, but this is what millions of people are experiencing right now: not being allowed to go out and do their regular jobs.'

'Come on, Anne,' said George, who was doing star jumps, ten feet away. 'Don't let them distract you. It's only a short workout.'

'Oh, is it that Joe Wicks feller?' said Dick, peering at the tablet that was propped up against a bird's nest. 'He gets everywhere, doesn't he?'

21

Dick and Julian both stood up, looking around for where they'd left their trousers.

'Come on,' said Anne, briskly, snatching up their sleeping bags. 'We're not letting our standards slip just because of a bit of adversity. It's nice, once you start! Invigorating!'

'Ordering pizza isn't very planet-forward, I freely admit,' said Julian. 'And getting it delivered all the way to the island cost more than a weekend in Budapest.'

Dick was, as ever, happy to exercise – all the more so if it annoyed or inconvenienced Julian. So he joined in at once. Julian wandered around dithering for as long as possible, put on some cricket trousers and began to participate half-heartedly.

'Just an easy, quick workout,' said the voice from the tablet. 'For all ages – two to a hundred and two!'

Julian reached for his toes and felt a tight, tearing pain spring to life in the central meat of his right thigh. I can't fail this on literally the first move, he told himself. Keep going. Now, the man on the screen was swaying his hips from side to side, swinging his arms over his head.

Julian attempted a mild hula-hoop movement and felt a heaving creakiness all around his torso and lower back, that put him in mind of the sound a ship made in a disaster movie when the plucky chief engineer finally began to lose hope. I'm falling apart, he thought.

There was a scratch on his leg and, investigating his pocket, he found it contained a corkscrew. He stared at it (still hula-hooping), wondering where it had come from. I haven't drunk for weeks, he thought. Is there such a thing as sleep-boozing?

Then he recalled that he'd satisfied a midnight sugar

craving with a box of Marks and Spencer truffles, which he'd had to open via the corkscrew within his sleeping bag so as to arouse no suspicion. Feeling a wonderful sense of relief, he began running on the spot with wild abandon and flung the corkscrew over his shoulder.

There was a terrible yowl and a yelp, and suddenly everyone was looking at him.

'What did I do?' he asked. They all searched through the tangled grass and weeds on the battlements and found poor Timmy lying on his back, licking a bleeding scratch in his side.

'Oh, dear friend!' said Julian. 'I didn't mean it!'

He reached out to comfort Timmy, but the dog growled and showed his teeth, then limped away to tend the wound in private.

'You'd do anything to get out of exercising, wouldn't you, rotter?' Anne said. Her hands were on her hips as she said this, but she was still rotating them so as not to miss out on the exercise routine.

'How would you like it?' said George, holding up the corkscrew.

Julian backed away. 'Honestly, it was a horrible mistake.

You know I love the old rogue. I'll make it up to him, I promise.'

After assuring themselves that Timmy was not seriously or lastingly hurt, the others resumed the workout. Half to himself, Julian said, 'I'll just sit the rest of this one out. Dangerous business, this fitness lark. Ha ha.'

He saw the brutal energy they threw into their exercises. And the fury they had been all too ready to turn on him. He felt it himself – it *was* a strain not to be allowed to investigate the theft. It was right up their alley. But, no, they had to stay here. Do nothing. Put it out of their minds.

Boscombe, though . . . It rang a bell . . .

While he tried to locate this particular bell, Julian decided to go for a walk. It was a stunning spring morning, after all. If this was to be their home for a week or two . . . Or longer? No, surely not. He chuckled to himself. There was no way the lockdown could possibly go on much longer than a fortnight. It just wasn't feasible.

Either way, it would be good to explore the island anew after a few years' absence. One heard so much about 're-wilding', these days, and the deliberate cultivation of the forgotten corners of the British countryside, with all its wild flora and fauna.

Kirrin Island had never been *de*-wilded in the first place. Where could be wilder? Between the fallen masonry of the ancient castle, and the jagged spurs of limestone that defined the island, there was a profusion of lush vegetation where wild food could be discovered, and even potentially cultivated, if it came to that.

In the old days they had nearly always brought picnics of sandwiches and orange squash with them (not ginger beer, which all his London friends seemed to think he had been reared on). And, despite every holiday starting in the same spirit of exploration, soon enough they were always hiding from some dastardly personage and trying to get back to the mainland. In fact, there were chunks of this island he hardly knew at all.

Seeing it was low tide, Julian wandered out as far as he could. He looked back at the remarkably craggy, dark caves he wasn't sure he'd ever been in. He threw seashells at the rusty, protuberant metal spheres that showed at low tide. He enjoyed the cascading screams of the gulls and jumped over the drying patches of seaweed.

'Good to be alive,' he said inaudibly, to the wind. A gull swooped down to a rockpool for a morning snack. 'Lockdown or no, Dorset is beautiful.'

How will we manage life in lockdown, George wondered,
without tearing each other's heads off?

Then he saw Timmy, twenty yards further out, head down in the sand. Gnawing away at something.

'Timtim!' he called. 'You dear old thing. I'm terribly sorry about our little contretemps!' He walked closer, and saw Timmy had a little toy he was playing with. 'Timmy?' he said. 'Where did you find that?'

But Timmy was determined to keep it to himself. Whichever direction Julian came towards him, Timmy turned to face directly away. Julian even thought he heard a little growl.

'*Tim*my . . .' Julian admonished, laughing. But when he could nearly reach him the dog trotted away, with the toy in his mouth.

'That isn't like you,' Julian said. 'I wonder what that thing is. Timmy!'

But now Timmy was gone, splashing away over the sand in a wide arc that bent towards the shore, the toy consistently held as far away from Julian as possible.

Julian felt that he had perhaps seen that toy somewhere before, but – surely not. There was something at the back of his mind that wanted to be remembered. Now it was *two* little bells ringing.

Julian walked back to the shore quickly, and, with

the beauty of the day and Dorset itself, and the breeze blissfully ruffling the hair at the back of his neck, he soon forgot about Timmy and any bells that had been going off in his head.

'They'll have finished their exercise by now,' he told himself. 'I wonder if I can persuade them it's not too early for lunch . . .'

But suddenly his thoughts were arrested by a third mystery. A very distinct and undeniable one, in front of him in the sand.

A single footprint, in the gap between two waves of the advancing tide, which had washed away its brothers and sisters. Only moments old, and already losing its definition in the wet sand. Julian looked around, the hair on the back of his neck suddenly impervious to the ruffling breeze. But he saw nothing in either direction.

CHAPTER FOUR

Elder Care

'Mummy,' said George. 'I'm so glad I caught you.'

'Oh yes, darling,' said Aunt Fanny. 'It's so wonderful to hear your voice. And to know you're so near.'

'Yes, you too,' George said. 'I loves ya, you know that.'

'Well, of course!' said Fanny.

'But I worry about you. Whether you appreciate how important it is to stay at home. And not to interact with other people?'

'. . . Yes, darling. I understand.'

'Do you?' George asked. 'It's just – I don't know how to make you realize how serious this is. It's really serious. And I love you so much. I don't want anything to happen to you.'

'Of course. I . . . I understand. Really, I do. *Thanks* for phoning.'

'What's that pause that keeps happening?'

'Sorry. I'm just taking tickets because I'm volunteering

at the old cinema in Wareham. You remember? They're having a screening of *Far From the Madding Crowd*. The old one. With Julie Christie – so beautiful. Not that I think the recent version is bad *at all*. Carey Mulligan can do no wrong, in my book!'

'Mum!' said George. 'Far from the madding crowd is where *you* should be! And all your friends! Honestly, this is not a joke, Mummy! It's really serious!'

'Oh, I'm sorry to alarm you, darling. Now, listen. I do understand. This was just an old commitment I had to fulfil. We're raising money for a new roof. I promise to stand at the very back of the screening, and leave straight after Terence Stamp get's shot. Spoiling alert! And I'm washing my hands every five minutes.'

'Thank you,' said George. 'I love you.'

'Love you too,' said Aunt Fanny. 'Got to go – it's time for me to take the ice creams round ...'

For hours afterwards, George couldn't keep still. It was hell, knowing that her mum was throwing herself, and so cheerfully, into such peril. When she calculated that the screening had ended, she waited for enough time to pass for her mother to get home, then phoned again.

'Darling,' said Fanny, answering the phone. It was hard

to make her out, because there was so much wind on the microphone.

'Mummy? Where are you?'

'You'll be pleased with me, darling – I'm miles from anyone or anything!'

'You're shouting,' said George. 'What exactly are you up to?'

'Overcoming my fear of heights!' Fanny said. 'Just like you told me to. In fact, I'm using up that voucher you bought me for a skydive! Don't worry – my instructor's strapped to my back. Do you want to say hello? He's called Roman!'

'Hullo,' said a voice.

'Mummy!' George yelled. 'Stop it! Go home and stay there!'

'WOOOOOOOOOOHHOOOUGH!' came a distant, tremulous voice through the phone. 'Wow! There goes the chute! Oh, this *is* exhilarating. Quite a breeze, though. We seem to be going off course. Where do you think we're going to set down, Roman?'

There was a manly murmur.

'He's afraid we might end up landing on the pitch of the local football club! How exciting! And, look! There's a game on!'

'This island must about in nuts and berries and roots – all freely available. And, you know, vegan or whatever.'

George disconnected, feeling light-headed. She took a few dozen deep breaths, went for a walk and then phoned back, nearly fainting when she discovered that Weymouth F.C. had scored in the moments before Fanny appeared out of the sky, and that the crowd had naturally taken her to be both a blessing and a lucky mascot.

'They call it "crowd-surfing", dear,' said Fanny. 'I was

so high with adrenaline, I couldn't help myself. I even snogged the referee!'

'The referee?' George wailed. 'You shouldn't be touching anyone!'

'Well, they all wanted one,' said Fanny. 'But he was a bit older, I thought that was more age appropriate. Oh! I'm getting my breath back, now, a bit, since they've put me down. Yes, boys! Calvin, Ollie, Abdulai, Jake! You're all my favourite! Yes, I'll be back next week! (Don't worry, George, I won't.)'

'But you *will* go home now,' said George, almost in tears. 'You promise me? Please! I really mean it!'

'Yes. Yes, I will,' said Fanny.

There was no easy sleep for George that night. She lay in exhaustion and torment while being visited by occasional terrors.

In the morning, before it was acceptable to call, she was on the phone to her mother again.

'Beautiful, isn't it?' Fanny asked.

'Yes, Mummy,' said George. 'Now, I want you to stay in the house today. And get used to being there for a while. It's for your own g— What's that noise?'

'What noise?' Fanny asked.

'It's something like a motor. A . . . Are you near a motorboat?'

'If you don't mind, I've got to change into my swimming outfit now. We're about to start, so I'll ring off.'

'You can't be serious,' said George, and was cross when she heard her mother huff with impatience. 'Start what?'

'The over-seventies all-Dorset formation synchronized water skiing, of course! I've told you about that.'

'*No.*'

'Now listen. No one's ever managed to form a diamond before. The Cornwall team tried last year, but then their star performer got caught in a propeller during the *Penzance Regatta* – a terrible business.'

'*MUM!*' George screamed. 'Go home! Now!'

Finally, something in her tone got through to Fanny. 'Why? What is it?' she asked.

George saw that this was her one chance, and that it might be fleeting. 'Get back to the house at once,' she said. 'It's Daddy.'

It was awful scaring her mum like this, but it just might save her life. Luckily, George knew that the jetty the team used was only a hundred-yard dash from Kirrin Cottage.

'Okay, I'm indoors,' Fanny said. 'What is it?'

'Daddy's downstairs in his laboratory, right?'

'Of course,' said Fanny. 'As always.'

'Go down and make sure.'

George heard the sound of her mother breathlessly rushing down the stairs. 'He's here! He's snoozing at his desk! What should I do?'

In the background, George heard a startled Quentin ask, 'What? What's going on? I was just resting my eyes . . .'

'He's okay,' said Fanny. 'Oh, thank God. Is he in danger?'

'Mummy,' said George, 'I want you to repeat after me: "At last we meet, Professor Kirrin!"'

'"At last we meet, Professor Kirrin!"? What is this? I shall repeat no such thing.'

'And now say, "I am your nemesis, Professor Kuragin!"'

'If this is a joke,' Fanny said, rapidly sobering, 'Then it isn't very funny.'

'What the devil is going on?' Quentin asked, in the background.

'Say it,' George insisted.

'The whole team of the Dorset Silver Surfers are waiting for me,' said Fanny. 'I don't know what makes you think you can trick me into saying something as stupid as "I am your nemesis, Professor Kuragin!"!'

In the background, George caught a brief auditory glimpse of her father panicking and telling Fanny to stop speaking, then a loud siren sounded, immediately overwhelmed by the noise of heavy machinery. And the line went dead.

'My God,' George said, sitting down in relief, looking pale.

'What was all that bollocks?' said Julian, who had given up going back to sleep.

'My mum,' said George. 'To explain, my dad told me once, in a moment of self-reflection, that he only had one equal in the world, one individual he feared.'

'Your mum,' said Julian.

'Don't be stupid. No: a Soviet scientist called Kuragin. Dad had a security system installed in case the man ever came to try and trick him into revealing his secrets. And that was the key phrase.'

'"I am your nemesis, Professor Kuragin!"? Doesn't sound like anything any self-respecting evil scientist would bother actually saying,' said Julian, plumping up his pillow.

'No. But, as I just proved, it works as a trick phrase. Sounds so stupid, you can say it aloud yourself in a parodic context, or trick someone else into saying it.'

'So, your ma and pa are both locked down? In his laboratory?'

'Good and proper. Until the only other person with a key comes to give the all-clear that crucial national secrets are no longer at risk.'

'And that person is?'

'MI-6.'

'The Tom Cruise film, or the British intelligence network?'

George just sighed.

'They've got food and water?'

'Water-purifier fixed to the cistern, and twenty years' worth of supplies freeze-dried and stored during the Cuban Missile Crisis. In many ways, they're better off than us. And it might finally do some actual good to their bloody marriage.'

'Win, win, win,' said Julian. 'Good work, dear girl.'

George nodded, and even allowed herself to smile, just a little bit. 'Thanks,' she said.

'Now, bugger off and let me sleep,' said Julian.

CHAPTER FIVE

The Wild Hunt

Julian crouched in absolute silence as the bunny crossed the grass in front of him. He didn't move a hair, nor dare to breathe.

The unwitting prey looked around, seemed to nod to itself, and took a few steps further. It was now agonizingly close to the trap Julian had laid in the grass. But had stopped just short of it. Sniffed. Thought some more. Cocked its head on one side. Inched nervously forward . . . Behaved, in general, like a nervous criminal about to be caught.

Which is exactly what you bloody are, thought Julian. You delicious bastard.

A raven cawed as it came to land in a nearby tree. The bunny looked towards it – so did Julian – Julian looked back – the bunny was gone.

He launched himself from his hiding place within an elderflower bush with a roar of anger and frustration, yanking the cord to close the trap on his escaped prey. The bird looked down on him.

'Yes, that's my cousin,' said George.

Julian turned to discover he was in the background of George's shot, in her work meeting. Even from six feet away, and in a small square in the corner of a screen, he could see how unconvincing his face paint and camouflage were. No wonder the Beast had escaped. Unable to contain his rage, he swatted the air with his improvised trap (a noose, fashioned from an extension cord, dangling on the end of a selfie stick), snarled and flailed away into the brush.

'Yes,' George said to her screen. 'Yes, he is. Yes, it's very sad. Nearly forty. No. We do our best to look after him . . .'

Julian found a muddy puddle that reflected the stunningly empty sky and zhooshed up his markings a bit. More on the forehead and cheekbones, he reckoned, ought to do it. He also tightened the headband and put some extra grasses, twigs and flowers in it. (After all, flowers – why not?) He wished that destiny had bestowed upon him a more useful garment for his upper body than the cricket jumper he had guilelessly popped into his rucksack when

*'He was embarrassed to find that he'd walked into
the background of his sister's work meeting.'*

packing for the island. Still, needs must. The whole thing was already thoroughly bedaubed with muck and grime, but, with the first coat starting to dry, he now gave it a second and a third coat to really freshen it up. After all, experience had shown him that he had to be at his best to catch the Beast.

Some might laugh at his efforts – let them! They did not fully understand the creature's cunning, its intelligence. Whenever he caught sight of it, Julian was transfixed. The sleek majesty of the animal as it moved, the muscles rippling beneath its fur.

But then, he had skipped breakfast. With an effort of will Julian had forced himself to stop imagining its skinned flesh browning over a flame, bubbling with juices, fat spitting and herbs adding their smoky flavour. He mustn't think about it as food. Nor as prey. Instead, he allowed its mind and his to be in harmony, so they were moving as one.

Where would *he* go next, if he were the Beast? Yes, down to the water's edge, of course. He felt it.

Julian was skipping across the castle ramparts to the steep downward path when he was arrested by two heads – those of Anne and Dick – appearing over a nearby wall.

'Do you *mind*?' said Dick. 'I'm on a work call! Really, Julian, you are most selfish!'

'Well,' said Julian, stopping short. 'I'm sorry.'

'We're trying to get work done!' said Anne. 'You're not the only person on this ruddy island, you know!'

'Was I . . . er . . . making a bit of noise?'

'You know full well you were. You were yelling at the top of your lungs. And I don't know if that Native American battle cry of yours is cultural appropriation or not, but, either way, it is most inappropriate!'

'Right, well . . . Sorry, I . . .'

Both heads disappeared and a somewhat subdued Julian continued making his way down to the beach. Behind him, he could hear Anne saying to a colleague of hers, 'Yes. Yes, he is. Yes, it's very sad. Nearly forty . . .'

But Julian wasn't listening. Instead, he was prowling through the tall grass, sniffing, examining the earth and waiting for a sign of his quarry. Happening to glance up at the castle, he saw a familiar shape silhouetted against the sky. Plump, juicy. Front paws raised as it nibbled some grass.

'Clever bastard,' he said through gritted teeth. 'You win this round . . .'

'So!' said Anne, closing her laptop and smiling up at him brightly. 'What's for lunch?'

This was a particularly sharp, sarcastic cheerfulness Julian had started to notice his sister using, when she fully expected to be disappointed. She *is* turning into Mother, he thought.

That morning, tension in the Kirrin party had gone up a notch at the news that, during the preceding night, a large and important consignment of toilet paper had been seized by a lone gunman, who had commandeered the lorry by a warehouse in Poole. This left several major towns and cities in Dorset, plus surrounding countryside, amounting to nearly a million people, severely compromised, not to say thoroughly uncomfortable.

And, for Dorset's prime amateur detectives, it was nearly impossible to take. Once again, they were not allowed to investigate. They could not do anything. They *were supposed to do nothing*. This was lockdown life, impossible as it seemed.

It had been agreed, on their second night on the island, that they ought to take it in turns to organize dinner. Dick having served up on the first night, Anne and then George had been chosen next.

The two women had, in Julian's view, utterly cheated by rowing to the mainland and then driving to the shops. Civilization, it seemed, had not crumbled during the first forty-eight hours of lockdown, and there was still some food to be bought.

When it came to Julian's turn, they explained that he was on his own. They refused to buy things for him and transport them back, owing to some unfortunate remarks he had apparently made about women drivers at some point. Typical of them to remember!

He couldn't go on his own because he wasn't insured on Dick's car, which (in truth) was just as well, because he was banned from driving anyway, a circumstance which he didn't care to be forced to explain. And so, having refused either to purchase supplies from Anne and George at a galling markup or to offer a 'grovelling apology', he was on his own.

Forced on to his own ingenuity. Which was a good thing! The island would provide. He knew it.

In the morning, Julian had attempted to hunt the bunny that lived somewhere near their encampment.

Julian was beguiled by rosy imaginings of Samwise Gamgee and Frodo enjoying a feast of coney stew, just a

'We don't even know if the Co-op in Dorchester will be open!'

stone's throw from Mordor. But, when it came to catching the Beast, Tolkien was irritatingly short on details. And, of course, the moment Julian started actively looking for it, it was nowhere to be seen. That was when he had got the first inkling of its devilish ingenuity . . .

Julian had whiled away most of the morning stubbornly proving that he was unable to catch rabbits by hand, meaning that, at lunch, facing up to his maddeningly cheerful sister, he was forced to part with the last of his own supplies: a tube of salt and vinegar Pringles, several assorted cup-a-soups, two oat bars, a white-chocolate Twix and a 'rucksack-matured' South West Trains egg bap.

It might be short commons, but Julian felt that, when it came to condiments, he really was a handsome provider. He never left a fast-food restaurant without scooping up anything that was free, edible and in sealed packaging. Thanks to this habit, the island now had a pretty decent supply of soy sauce, mustard, malt vinegar, ketchup, brown sauce, sugar, milk, coffee biscuits, wasabi paste, and peri-peri sauce – both 'Mild' and 'Vesuvian'.

Dick, a schoolboy at heart, was perfectly happy as he squeezed year-old brown sauce on to his quarter of the egg bap, and topped it with crunched-up Pringles. But the girls proved harder to please.

'Lemsip for pudding?' Julian asked, waving several de-crumpled sachets. 'I've got some water boiling.'

'Nah, bruv,' said George.

'Certainly not,' said Anne. 'And, when dinner time comes, we would like some *dinner*, by the way. Is that clear?' And she turned her back, booting up her laptop with a sigh.

CHAPTER SIX

Hunter S. Gatherer

In the afternoon, decidedly bucked up by a delicious Lemsip, Julian returned to the hunt.

During lunch break, his philosophy had matured.

Okay, he thought. Owing to the unnatural shackles of modern life and so-called morality, I may have been deprived of the instinct to be a hunter. But, by God, I'll prove to the world I'm one *hell* of a gatherer.

And then he had a brainwave.

He fumbled in his pocket for his phone, and then nervously searched through his contacts list. The number was still there. He dialled, and then prayed for a signal.

'Hello?' said a voice.

'Andy!' Julian gasped. 'Andy! Thank God you answered!'

'You all right, mate? May I ask who this is?'

The previous summer, Anne and Dick had bought Julian a 'booze foraging' experience near Dorchester. The idea

49

was for a picturesque ramble showing which pickable plants one could use to complement, or flavour, alcoholic drinks. Or something like that. Julian had got rather into the spirit of things ahead of time and the walk itself was a bit of a blur. However, what he *had* retained was (choirs in heaven rejoice) the phone number of Andy Hamilton, the foraging expert.

'Oh, right, yeah,' said Andy. 'You want a few pointers?'

'Please,' said Julian. 'You don't know how grateful I'd be!'

There seemed to be a little hesitance at first from Andy's end, and he asked a few times whether Julian 'remembered how that night had ended', but his natural enthusiasm soon took control.

'A place like Kirrin Island, you'll have wild garlic,' he said. 'You can eat the flowers, shoots and bulbs of that. Burdock, too. Just the roots though.'

'Wild garlic,' said Julian, as he walked along, through a grassy swathe of land, analysing it with new eyes. 'I can look it up on Google Images.'

He felt like he had Terminator vision, but for edible plants.

'Nettles,' said Andy. 'You recognize those. There'll

be lots of those around, and you can cook them. A great source of nutrients.'

'Nettles!' said Julian. 'An enemy, turned into food!'

'Then there's common hogweed,' said Andy. 'Don't confuse it with giant hogweed, which grows near water and burns your skin. With common hogweed, what you

'Eff this effing intranet portal!' said Anne. 'It only works at a tenth the speed it should!'

want to do is pick as low down the stem as you can, and get it just before the leaves uncurl and grow hairier.'

'Before the leaves uncurl,' Julian repeated. He was quickly backtracking to the camp, where he could make some notes.

'That's correct. The leaves are shaped like cats' paws. But you want to get them before they *start* to uncurl.'

Julian was determined to succeed. He nodded, writing this down. Some stubborn part of his mind forced him to ask, 'How do I detect the leaf that is about to uncurl? What signs does it give of its . . . *incipient* decurling?'

'Look at the leaves,' said Andy. 'If they're curly, you're good to go.'

'Of course. Must cook it through.'

'Then there's lime leaves. You'll have those on the island, I expect.'

'I expect so too. Now, those are quite unrelated to the fruit, are they not?'

Andy laughed loudly. 'You're funny, Julian. I'd forgotten you were funny.'

'Thanks. But they're *not* though, are they?'

'From the lime tree,' said Andy, laughter still in his voice. 'Good to eat as part of a salad. Then there's

Jack-by-the-hedge,' he continued. 'Grows in those parts. Found by a hedge, obviously, and on old wasteland. Mostly beside disturbed earth.'

Julian cast his eyes around. That described every inch of the whole island. He was starting to have serious doubts about his ability to put Andy's instructions to good use. But he didn't know quite what to ask in order to overcome his uncertainty.

'Dandelion roots, ivy-leafed toadflax,' Andy chirruped. 'Japanese knotweed shoots, at this time of year – they look like shoots of asparagus and taste like rhubarb.'

'Rhubarb,' said Julian. 'Well, what can I say? I'm terribly grateful. Really, I am. Next time I see you, the drinks are on me.'

'Next time you see me,' Andy replied happily, 'you owe me forty quid for what you did to that taxi.'

'Oh,' said Julian, sitting down on a stone wall. 'I'm really sorry.'

'Not at all,' said Andy. 'I've never seen anyone as angry as that cab driver. It's making me laugh just thinking about it. Good luck. Don't starve!'

Julian disconnected the call, feeling more alienated than ever from nature, and the idea of subsisting as a forager.

He had a sense that, with the leisure of a couple of days' googling and a very expensive colour printer, followed by great deal of trial and error, he had a fifty-fifty chance of putting together an edible side dish for a very hungry and unpicky vegan, albeit mixed in among lots of entirely inedible foliage. With crunched-up Pringles sprinkled over the top.

Mustn't be defeatist, though, he told himself. That's not how hunters think. Nor probably gatherers either. He still had several hours before dinner.

After all, said a voice in the back of his head, didn't the whole populace used to fast? Like, more than a hundred days per year? And felt great because of it? People said it was terribly good for your body and your clarity of mind . . . Even he had to admit, though, that that was a hard argument to make, after he had served up such a lame lunch. It smacked of the genuine desperation he was feeling.

Julian was wandering beneath the castle, through the wild grass, looking for nettles. Aren't most grasses edible? he wondered. Isn't there, like, a loaf of bread's worth of wheat from different grasses on this island, if I bothered gathering it . . .

'Bully for you,' said George. *'I've finished* The Well of Loneliness, *so I'm going to watch* Buffy *from the beginning. Again.'*

He realized that if there was, and the only animal capable of gathering it was . . .

Yes! Why had he not thought of it before? Goat!

Unless he was quite mad, or had dreamt it, he was sure that he had seen a goat on the island. A wild, ragged, shaggy thing. He hadn't given it a second thought at the time. There was a fifty-fifty chance that it was female. And, if so . . .

Well, the mind boggled.

Goat's milk. Goat's milk cheese. Goat's milk butter! Was there such a thing? Probably! He was determined to find out. And if the goat proved to be male, or a particularly difficult female . . . goat mutton!

Only a few moments later, Julian was climbing the island's one substantial hill, and not long thereafter had set eyes on the goat.

Julian bared his teeth. Let battle commence. God, this was primal.

It's not necessary, or particularly dignified, to go into detail about what happened in the next hour – the roaring and charging, the none-too-subtle sidling, the hiding and leaping out, the begging and pleading, the fury and futility of it all. By the end, Julian lay on his back, staring at the sky, his hands, like his mind, utterly empty. The goat, indifferent to his brush with fate, grazed nearby.

He had passed through despair to laughter, and was now in some indeterminate state. He finally felt he knew what the phrase 'shagged out' meant. He wondered what Joe Wicks would have made of his efforts. Probably, he thought, he would have had a hernia from laughing.

Julian got to his feet. He was still determined to find dinner, but the flesh was no longer willing. On his way back to camp, he tripped on a root, fell into a bush and found himself looking down at a nest full of eggs. The only protein he'd succeeded in discovering on his hunt. They were so exquisitely vulnerable and beautiful, he started to sob.

'No way,' said Anne.

'No WAY!' said Dick.

'Your reputation,' said George, 'has had a reprieve at the gallows. You wonderful genius.'

'They're not exactly warm,' said Julian, his voice still trembly from weeping. 'But, by God, they're good.'

'You never cease to amaze me,' said Anne. 'Honestly, you do. How, but *how*, did you get Domino's to deliver out here?'

'It is a tale of endurance, tenacity and cold hard lucre.'

'I suspect lucre is the lead instrument in this arrangement,' said Dick, supporting a slice on the tips of his fingers and angling it towards the food hole. 'Want to go into details?'

'Not really,' said Julian. 'Let's just eat. After hunting high and low for edible meat on this island, I found only one elusive bunny, whose destruction is my life's aim. There is also an adorable goat, whose life I could not bring myself to harvest. I knew you'd be with me on that.'

'Amen, sister,' said George.

'Bravo!' said Dick.

'I got stuffed crust as well,' said Julian. 'And chicken thingummies. All three types. Dips too. It didn't seem the time to stint. Plus coleslaw, for, like, one of five-a-day.'

'I don't know who Domino is, but I really hope he's bloody pleased with himself,' said Dick.

'It's not just Domino who deserves our gratitude. There's also the local owner of the military-strength drone that flew our dinner out to the coast, and a local fisherman who rowed it to the island, both of whom were at leisure and financially flexible. All in all, this meal cost more than a weekend in Budapest.'

'Worf ick,' said Anne, through a mouthful of dough.

'Agreeg!' said Dick.

'It's not very planet-forward, I freely admit,' said Julian. 'In fact, I've found some good tips on how to make us entirely self-sufficient on this island. And make us more vegan-facing.'

Julian watched his loved ones chewing away on the cheesy meaty dough like angry dogs. He was himself so weakened and hungry, and grateful and satisfied by pizza, he started weeping again.

'Woof,' said Timmy, putting his head in Julian's lap, the bone of a chicken thingummy sticking out of his mouth.

CHAPTER SEVEN

Time Lords

A light breeze fluted through the castle's arches and turrets. The midday sun beamed down hard and, all around, the colours of nature shone magnificently on Kirrin Island. Birds sang and choirs of insects made the sort of indefinable scratching, rasping noises that presumably meant they were up to something or other. (Probably having it off.)

'Eff this effing load of old effing B.S.!' said Anne.

'*Anne!*' said George, looking up, shocked.

Dick refused to be roused by this. He had his giant earphones on, so that the sides of his head looked like they were being snogged by giant plastic hoops.

'I'm sorry,' said Anne. 'It's this intranet. It works a tenth of the speed it should. And keeps logging me off. I've spent half a day trying to change one paragraph.'

'I was just shocked that you were being so prudish,' said George. 'If you want to swear, just swear. No one cares. We're on an island.'

'It's so frus*trating*,' Anne said palely. 'I might as well do all my work in the evening and upload it then, because currently I'm doing everything in triplicate!'

'Do that, then,' said George. 'You'll probably do it better.'

'But we're supposed to work in the day,' said Anne. 'I don't know what I'd do with myself. You and Dick are hard at work.'

'*I'm* not,' said George. 'I'm watching YouTube skate-board videos.'

'Me neither,' said Dick, carefully unpeeling his ears from their giant smacking lips. 'I'm playing Minecraft. Old skool.'

'Aaargh!' came a voice from the distance.

'I suppose that does seem sensible,' said Anne. 'After all, if I'm just wasting time, I might as well be doing something helpful or pleasurable . . .'

'Did I hear you saying "old skool", Dick?' said Julian, from the other side of a stone wall. 'It's intolerable! And I bet you spelled it with a *k*!'

'Are we interrupting you?' asked George.

'Yes,' came Julian's voice. 'I was just in the middle of a particularly complex chapter.'

'Oh, God,' said Dick. 'Don't get him started. Quick! Look busy!' He let go of his headphones so they reconnected to the sides of his head with a conjoined leathery smack.

'Chapter of what?' asked Anne.

'Your funeral!' Dick warned.

Julian stood up from his laptop, stretched and strolled over. He was wearing a white sheet, tied at the shoulder, like Julius Caesar, along with dark glasses and a tea towel round his head.

'It's a novel I pick up and put down every few years,' he said languidly. 'Probably rubbish, of course, but they say everyone's got a book in 'em. Most should stay there, I daresay! Ha ha!'

'Oh, Julian, you are clever,' said Anne. 'I wish I was so brave.'

'Well,' said Julian, sun reflecting off his shades, 'I wouldn't say I was *brave*, exactly . . .'

'Julian, you awful *twat*,' said George. 'If someone came at you spouting this sort of drivel, you'd run a mile. Why can't you use this furlough time for something useful?'

'Oh, Julian, were you furloughed, after all? That *is* such beastly luck.'

'It's easy for Julian to say we won't starve,' thought Anne.
'It'd take him a month longer than the rest of us!'

'Yes,' he said. 'Well, I presumed I was, anyway, after the pyjama incident. I can't ever look those people in the face again, so I shall just draw my salary until it stops and then look at my options after the lockdown.'

'What's your awful novel called, anyway?' asked George.

'*The Griefbacon of Ptolemmy Windpepper*,' said Julian.

This drew guffaws from the rest of the group (even Dick, sneakily listening in), who congratulated Julian on stringing them along. Julian, ever ready to adapt to circumstances, conceded that, yes, indeed, his novel was a terribly good joke. He made a mental note to alter the title.

'Now's the time, finally, to read that important book one's always been putting off,' said Anne. 'Really, it is – there'll never be a time like this.'

'Good idea,' said Dick. 'What was it that Dad always said we should read?'

'*The Day of the Jackal*,' said Julian. 'A man's book. That, or *Rogue Male*.'

'Oooh, Julian,' Anne cooed. 'You really must read *Shantaram*. I read it when I was on holiday in Sri Lanka. It's *such* a good read.'

'My darling girl,' said Julian, 'thanks for your

recommendation, but I was thinking more along the lines of the complete text of Gibbon's *Decline and Fall*, or the unexpurgated Pepys.'

'Bully for you,' said George. 'I've finished *The Well of Loneliness*, so I'm going to watch *Buffy* from the beginning. Again.'

'Ah, yeah, I'm up for that, G!' said Dick. 'Can I join in? I was too young for it, first time round. As for reading, I was thinking of doing Discworld from start to finish. The definition of an enjoyable project, right?'

'Julian,' said Anne, 'if you are intending to download those texts on to my Kindle, I suggest you start being nicer to me. I was under the impression you were looking forward to reading only Dickens while you were on the island.'

'Dickens and I,' said Julian, 'have come to an arrangement.'

Anne narrowed her eyes, examining her poseur brother standing there in the sunshine, unsure if he was trying to quash any further questions, or invite them. On the whole, she couldn't be bothered to find out.

'What,' she said, tossing him her Kindle, 'evs.' She picked up her sunglasses and reached for her sun lotion. 'Read all you like, nerdface. I'm going to get some rays.'

CHAPTER EIGHT

The Julian Calendar

Each of the Kirrins spent much of the rest of that day by themselves, guiltily exploring a leisure activity despite the fact that they were on someone's payroll. They were only called together again towards dinner time, when George had an emergency.

'It's my future employers,' she said. 'They want to talk to me.'

'Okay,' said Dick. 'What's the problem?'

'They don't know I live on a damn island, in the open air!' she said. 'I've told them I'm in lockdown in London. And I said yes to a video call before I knew what I was doing.'

'Okay,' said Dick again. 'So email them back—'

'They're calling in ten minutes,' said George. She was pacing forward and back, running her hands through her hair. 'I can't be caught lying to them like this. Not in our first face-to-face discussion!'

Finally, here was something that called upon the concerted invention of the whole group.

'Dick, could you pick some flowers, and I'll put them in this bottle,' said George. 'Thanks. Julian, can I borrow that paperback, for set dressing? Anne, what do you think we could use for a backdrop?'

'I've got one ready,' said Anne. 'Here.'

As she unfurled the old bedsheet Anne handed her, George gaped. It had been decorated to look like a patch of background wall. The attention to detail was extraordinary. There was a clearly defined skirting board, a double plug socket, and (it took George a few seconds to notice this) the blurry shadow thrown by an unseen hat stand, shaded with exquisite care.

'It's a masterpiece,' George said, watching as Dick and Julian hung it up.

'Yes,' said Anne, as she held up her mirror for George to give herself a once-over. 'Well, everyone likes Monet's *Water Lilies*. I had to work with what colours I had, and there was no time to do anything more adventurous.'

It was only as she said this that Dick and Julian got to the section of the sheet she was referring to. There,

'Someone's stolen Dorset's entire supply of hand sanitiser!'

on the sheet, Anne had recreated a perfectly credible and creditable replication of a Monet print.

'You're a genius!' said George.

'You're a loony,' said Julian. 'Why didn't you just do a Rothko? It wouldn't have taken five minutes.'

'I *did* do a Rothko,' said Anne, 'on the other sheet. I made two.'

'Two?' asked Dick, feeling weak.

Anne nodded. 'This one's for a south-facing room, the other for a west. That's how I thought of them, anyway.'

'When did you have the time?'

'We all find the time for what matters to us, Dick,' said Anne. 'For instance, *I* want to make sure my colleagues think the inside of my flat looks nice. So I found time for it. Like *you* found time to spend six days lying on the sofa, playing *Animal Crossing* on your Nintendo, but "couldn't get the time off work" to come to Greece with me for a long weekend.'

'There's no time for recriminations,' said Julian. 'Look at George's laptop – they're calling through now!'

George made a sort of despairing grunt, checked in the mirror one last time to make sure she looked suitably manly, plumped herself in front of the laptop and got ready to take the call.

'Anne, be my housemate?' George asked. 'Wander across the back of the shot looking gorgeous, and then back the other way, two minutes later?'

'Breathe,' said Dick, handing her a glass of water. 'You'll be fine. They've already hired you!'

George gave Dick a grateful peck on the cheek, which made both of them blush slightly. Then she looked around at her beloved cousins, all looking on with consternation.

'Stop staring, freaks.'

Then she clicked her touchpad. 'Hi!' she said to the screen. 'How are you guys?'

Anne, Dick and Julian flumped on the ground nearby, exhausted, but still alert for any emergency that might arise.

'Well done on the calendar, Julian,' said Dick. 'That was an inspired addition.'

'Just as long as they don't look too closely,' he replied. 'It's for 1944.'

The others turned to look at him.

'I found a rather interesting cache today, in one of

the caves, while the tide was out,' Julian explained. 'It must have been left by some Second World War soldiers. No doubt they were out here on exercises or training or something. A notepad, a radio set, some tins of bully beef. Even a crate of gin!'

'Wow! You should bring it back here, to camp,' said Anne.

'What do you think I was doing for two hours before this? It's all stashed. And that calendar was part of it. As was this,' said Julian, producing an armful of fabric. 'An unused parachute. Anne, weren't you saying yesterday that you wished you had fabric so you could make face masks? After all those hospital supplies got stolen yesterday, you said they'd published patterns online for people to make their own at home. You've got your sewing kit, right? What could be more patriotic!'

'Julian, you're a genius,' she said.

'Wait a minute,' Dick said. 'Someone *stole* hospital supplies?'

Anne nodded. 'Three lorries' worth. Carjacked, coming down the road from Burton Bradstock. At gunpoint!'

'That's *three* local crimes we could have investigated,' said Dick.

'I know,' said Julian. 'It's impossibly frustrating. I wonder if the crimes could be connected in some way?'

'Hey, Anne, it's time for your appearance,' said Dick.

The two brothers were impressed by the nonchalance with which Anne wandered into the back of the shot.

'She's killing it,' said Dick.

Then Anne appeared to have a thought. 'Timmy!' she called. And the faithful old dog bounded into view, nuzzling Anne's hand before going to rest his head in George's lap.

'Killing it,' agreed Julian as Anne wandered out of shot in the opposite direction. 'Look at her. Model. Actress. Set designer. My sister.'

'Yes, I love animals, I really do. I love them so much,' George was saying to the screen. And Timmy looked up adoringly at her, very much seconding her sentiment.

But then George appeared strained. 'Excuse me?' she asked. 'The connection isn't great. Could you repeat that?'

They did so. It still sounded like they had said something about a bloody goat. It seemed an odd choice of words.

'Ba-a-a-a,' complained a recognizably animal voice.

George, as casually as possible, turned to glance behind her. There, a shaggy-haired animal had limped into camp

72

and was huddled against the backdrop sheet. There was a splash of vivid red across its fur by the neck. The poor thing seemed to be injured and struggling to breathe. Timmy yelped and dashed for safety.

'Ah,' George said cheerfully. Her cousins watched with pained expressions as she tried to style it out. 'There's my goat. Yes. Yes, he is bleeding. I probably ought to see to him in a moment. But don't stop with your questions . . .'

At this point, the goat appeared to experience some breathing difficulty. It coughed twice, very noticeably decorating the backdrop sheet with speckles of blood, and then collapsed, causing the sheet to fall on to it, and revealing the castle wall behind.

'____,' said Timmy.

CHAPTER NINE

G.O.A.T.

The good thing about being English, George reflected, was that, when something went wrong, nobody bloody messed around with such things as sympathy. There was nothing George hated in this world more than sympathy.

As her potential employers terminated the call, Julian walked over to her and said, 'Not got that job, then?'

'No, it seems not,' said George.

'Bloody goat swung it?' asked Julian.

'I'd say so. PETA are real sticklers about that sort of thing.'

'Ah. Is that who you were . . . ? Oh well. Terribly bad luck. Buck up!' He punched her on the shoulder in an affectionate way, then went over to the goat.

'Bloody thing's alive!' he said.

After that, there was no time for self-pity. George was delighted and excited by the prospect of something being saved from the destruction of her future career, and fought hard to keep the goat's wound (which was deep, but not arterial) clean and bandaged, and the animal supplied with water. The idea that someone had recklessly harmed it infuriated her nearly as much as the idea that hospital supplies had been stolen. ('At gunpoint!' Anne kept saying.) First the hand sanitizer, then the toilet paper. Now this.

'It's like some bastard's holding the whole county to ransom!' George said. And, like all the others, she felt a tingle of recognition. But she couldn't quite place it.

Soon, Anne and George were hard at work making face masks from the parachute material, and producing hand sanitizer by thoroughly mixing the gin with lubricant from a twelve-gallon tub, which they had agreed to tell themselves was Vaseline, but which they suspected might be machine grease.

Dick and Julian, meanwhile, had to keep their new friend the goat alive, and watered. It was a job they were proud to do.

'There you go, Goaty McGoatface,' said Julian. 'Delicious milk, delicious milk . . .'

'That's a stupid name,' said Anne.

'And disrespectful,' said George.

'What should we call him, then?' asked Dick.

The others looked at the injured goat, lying on the ground, with its head in Julian's lap. There was a lacuna.

'The Latin for goat is capra,' said Julian.

There was a general murmur of approval.

'But I think he looks more like a Neil,' said Julian. 'So that's what I'm going to call him.'

'Big udders for a Neil,' said Anne.

'I can't help but like females with male names,' said George.

'Neil it is,' said Dick.

'Stop talking and have a go on them nips would you,' said Julian. 'We might get some goat's cheese out of this.'

'I'm not sure this *is* gin, you know,' said Dick, looking at the unlabelled bottle after taking a swig. 'It has a schnapps-y taste to it.'

'Don't talk rot,' said Julian. 'I know good English gin when I taste it.'

Anne, who was in the middle of making a cup of tea for everyone, suddenly stopped.

'Who did this?' Anne asked, looking up. 'There was an injury to its neck, wasn't there?'

No one answered.

'The other morning,' Julian admitted, 'when you were

'We bought some ox tongue from Waitrose. It was on special offer.'

'Posh a-holes.'

all at your laptops and I took Timmy for a run along the shore, there was . . .'

He paused. It sounded so stupid. He didn't want to say it.

'Evidence of other people on the island?' said a voice.

Everyone went still as a face emerged from the darkness.

'Peter!' growled Julian. He leapt up, and briefly staggered from the pain that shot across his shoulders, down his back, up his legs and buttocks, thanks to Joe Wicks. But luckily this just made his grimace meaner.

Dick leapt to his side, and then Anne and George came to stand behind them, grabbing the gnarliest weapons to hand (a tennis racket they'd been playing French cricket with and a pair of barbecue tongs, respectively). They needed all the physical and psychological weapons they could lay their hands on, while facing up to the superlatively slimy Peter, leader of the Secret Seven.

'Got the goat, did you?' said Peter, his nasal public-school prefect's voice giving the lie to the remarkably rock-hard abs on display as he stepped closer to them. 'What jolly good luck.'

The Kirrin party became aware of six other faces staring at them out of the darkness. Timmy growled.

'Barbara!' said George. 'You're still apologizing for this monster? I know you're better than this! You too, Janet!'

They all stopped at the perimeter of the camp, just visible in the firelight.

'*We're* being socially responsible,' said Barbara.

'We thought we had this island to ourselves,' said Peter, flexing his fatuous smile.

'Don't be an imbecile,' said Anne. 'This has always been our island. George's island, particularly. It *belongs* to her. Not you. The Secret Seven should stay out!'

'Yes,' said George. She couldn't quite summon the aggression the moment called for, because she was wrong-footed by the creepiness of all this. 'Go away, you nasty little bunch.'

'Oh, we were trying to stay out.' Peter smiled. 'We happened to be passing, and thought this was a sensible spot for self-isolating on the south coast. No rest for the wicked, though. There are always crimes to solve. You can do it all remotely these days, of course. Only a couple of cases this week – one in Manitoba, another in Senegal. With our leftover time, we've been idly brushing up on a few things: Janet's translating *The Taming of the Shrew* into Taiwanese; Jack's been working on his magic. Show them, Jack?'

Peter's best friend stepped forward, brandishing some cards. He asked Julian to pick one and look at it, then return it to the pack. He shuffled twice, and asked Julian whether he wanted a Flake.

'A Flake?' Julian asked. Then he realized he was holding an ice-cream cone. 'Jesus!' he said, dropping it, by accident, into the fire. 'How did you *do* that?'

The Secret Seven all applauded Jack's effort. The others did not.

'Yes, so we never intended to be here at all,' said Peter. 'Sheer coincidence. Congratulations on bagging our goat, by the way. Barbara shot it – with a bow she made herself, this morning. Good luck for you. Might have ended up a bit peckish without that, what?'

'Your congratulations are premature,' said Julian.

'And immature!' said George.

'We're perfectly capable of feeding ourselves,' said Julian.

Peter glanced at the pile of pizza boxes.

'Do hang it for five days before you eat it,' he said to

himself. 'Unless you like eating tough meat, of course. Never can tell with you country folk. Might want to think about cutting your hair soon, too. It's starting to look like *Scooby-Doo* round here.'

'Stuff off,' said Dick.

'Also – feel free to join me for t'ai chi on the beach at sunrise. That's 6.12 a.m. tomorrow.' He tickled the air with a five-finger exercise. 'Toodle-oo!' he said. 'I'm sure you're following the same leads we are. May the best team win . . .'

And, by the time the Kirrins had a chance to wonder what he was talking about with regard to leads, he had dissolved into darkness. Along with his teammates.

The effect was sinister, repulsive, and decidedly irritating.

CHAPTER TEN

On the Beach

The four Kirrins divided up their tasks for the rest of the day, but really they were mostly focused around nursing Neil. Here was a wild creature whose condition reflected badly on the Secret Seven and, if they'd had no other motivation for her survival, this would have been enough.

The four Kirrins plus Timmy ensured Neil's comfort, then went to wash in the sea, and on the way back home found themselves discussing their recent encounter.

'Really, Peter *is* such an odious worm,' said Anne. 'Whose turn is it to make dinner?'

'Mine,' said Dick. 'Right, Timmy?'

'Woof!' said Timmy, running ahead.

'You know,' Dick said, 'I'm not at all convinced those metal things with spikes, on the shore, aren't leftover Second World War mines.'

'Ha!' laughed Julian. 'That's hilarious. You feeble-minded old—'

'Yes,' said George. 'That's exactly what they are. They were missed by the crews who cleaned up such things after the war – probably because the island was thought uninhabitable. Defunct now, though, you'd expect.'

A frost spread throughout Julian's vitals at the thought that he had spent a whole afternoon lobbing rocks at those things, just two days ago. Normally, he would have been furious and shouted at George, but, at that moment, he couldn't breathe. Thank God for my appalling throwing arm, he thought. I owe it my life!

'What do you think he meant about following up leads?' asked George.

'Idle boasting,' said Dick.

But Julian, finally getting his breath back and keen to be thinking about anything else, demurred. 'That's what I was about to say, before he appeared. The other day, I saw a footprint on the beach. It was a Hunter's welly footprint. None of the Seven were wearing those – I looked.'

'They might have more than one set of shoes,' Anne said.

'Absolutely,' said Julian. 'But it's a steep climb to get up here in the dark, with thistles and so forth, you might tread on. If you've *got* wellies, you'd be mad not to use them.'

'So, what? There's someone else on the island?'

Julian shrugged. 'Maybe. All I know is that that creep said they were following up leads, which means that there's a moderate chance that is what they *are* doing. And, if there's a mystery on this island, I'm damned if I'm going to let the bloody Secret Seven solve it!'

'Me too!' said Anne. 'Or me neither. Whichever means I agree with you!'

'Bravo!' said Dick.

'Amen,' said George.

'Woof!' said Timmy.

CHAPTER ELEVEN

Lockdown Life

The five of them had returned to the camp fired up with enthusiasm. They were ready to get stuck into a new adventure – to achieve something good, together, again!

But nothing happened. They went to bed, they got up. They did exercise. They did work. They ate dinner. It was sunny.

The next day, the same. And the day after, and the day after. It became a dull ache, the monotony. It wasn't bad, it wasn't good. It was just the same. Nothing changed, except for the pile of face masks they sewed, together, in the evenings, while they watched TV.

As for the case: it was cold. They analysed the evidence and examined all the information to hand, but they could uncover no leads to follow up.

During the day, while the others worked, Julian explored the island, taking in the hill, every room of the castle, the beaches (keeping well clear of the spiked metallic balls), the caves. No further trace of the welly-wearer was forthcoming.

The Secret Seven kept their distance, as did that sumptuous Beast, the rogue bunny. Julian still caught sight of it now and then, but he had decided to take on a Zen attitude towards it.

And then one day they were walking out to perform the eight p.m. clap for the NHS, when Julian nipped back for his phone. The roar of anger rising up from the camp brought the rest of them running.

'It's all gone – look!' he said. 'The whole pile of facemasks that we made. They've stolen it all! Quick! The thief must have been just here! Aha!'

His torchlight picked out one figure in the corner of the camp. It was Peter, and he was stationed by a wide embrasure, in a position that would have been perfect for him to throw down supplies to someone standing below.

'"Aha!"? That's rather melodramatic, isn't it, Julian? Rather an old-fashioned line?'

'We *like* old-fashioned lines, here, on our island,' said George.

'And we'll say "aha" if we want to,' said Anne.

'Which we do,' said Dick.

'Exactly,' said Julian. 'AHA! Caught you bloody red-handed, you nasty little cheat. Stealing all the supplies *we've* made, because we're nice people, and hoping to take credit by rowing it to the mainland yourselves, I expect? You horrible little worm.'

'Must say, when I came for a little forage, I thought you'd have some more interesting reading material I might borrow,' said Peter, holding up what had once been a fat

'The next day was the same. And the day after that, and the day after that.'

paperback, but was now a shell, with nearly all its pages torn out. 'I can see Pickwick,' he continued, holding it up by one corner. 'But where, oh where, are his papers?'

'*Dickens and I,*' said Julian, through gritted teeth, '*have come to an arrangement.*'

'Ha!' said Peter. 'Well, I suppose that proves it wasn't you who stole the toilet paper, doesn't it?'

Julian was breathing very hard through his nose. And the colour of his face (although barely visible in the torchlight) was undergoing a rapid series of changes. Deepening, darkening, reddening, mottling. New pathways and pipe-lines of powerful rage, never before accessed by him, were opening up and going at full clank, and he was starting to wobble all over, as though turning into some kind of jelly. None of the others had ever seen anything like this in him before.

'You bloody swine, I'll kill you!' were the words that he had a vague plan of uttering, but what came out of him was more a kind of swirling animalistic howl.

Peter, of course, was a big lad – taller and naturally stronger than Julian. He looked after himself too, had abs all the way to Wednesday week and was highly proficient in a smattering of martial arts. But what he saw coming at him now was somehow outside all his training, a sort of mad scrambling beast with no logic to it. He took fright, and - crucially - hesitated.

Julian rugby-tackled him at the waist and they both disappeared clean out of the window, tumbling into the night.

Anne screamed. Dick and George looked out. There was a loud thump as the two men landed, and more shouting, with Peter begging Julian to see the funny side, and to calm down, and to stay two metres away from him at all times.

'Woof!' said Timmy. 'Woof! Woof, woof, woof!'

'He'll murder him!' said Anne. 'And break his own neck!'

'I think,' George reflected, 'that might genuinely be the way he wanted to go.'

'Better call an ambulance, just in case. If such a thing is possible,' said Dick. 'Which reminds me. Talking of the NHS: eight o'clock draws near . . .'

CHAPTER TWELVE

Mine! All Mine!

Anne, Dick, George and Timmy went down to the shore.
They weren't quite sure what else to do. After all, it was
the best place to get a phone signal.

As they got to the water's edge, in the failing light they
saw a figure backing out from the rocks on to the beach. It
was that of a middle-aged man, grey haired and bearded,
dressed in shabby clothing. He was angry and shouting
as two younger, more athletic figures advanced upon him.
They had all emerged from the same cave.

'Okay, okay!' he was saying. 'Stay back!'

'You think a Second World War Luger is going to fire,
after all these years?' Julian taunted him. Beside him stood
Peter. The two of them looked remarkably well, considering
the physical battering they had both recently gone through.

'Do you want to risk it?' asked the man.

Dick, George and Anne held their breath. They saw he
had a gun in his hand. They also recognized the voice.

'Rupert!' said Anne. 'Oh, you rotter!'

Rupert swivelled, then turned the gun back on Peter and Julian, who were advancing on him.

'Back!' he said. 'I'll shoot. I bloody will!'

'What the hell's going on?' asked George.

'He was in the dungeons,' said Julian. 'Hiding out there behind a fake wall. As I was chasing Peter we crashed into a wall and went straight through – it was made of plaster – and there he was. Our horrible creep of a cousin. He has it all down there – all the supplies of toilet roll, face masks and hand sanitizer for the whole of Dorset!'

Anne buried her face in her hands. It was too much to bear, that this awful man was their cousin. They had foiled him so many times before, and here he was now up to his old tricks!

'I should have known when I saw Timmy playing with that toy,' said Julian. 'That was Lily's special toy!'

'My wife chucked me out,' Rupert admitted, itching his unshaven chin with the butt of the pistol. 'That toy's all I've got to remember of dear Lily. For now.'

This reference left Peter at a loss.

'A few years ago,' Julian explained, 'we looked after

this git's daughter while he was in prison – for another crime we nabbed him for.'

'His beautiful daughter!' cried Anne. Dick put his arm round her.

'Yes, she was a belter,' said George. 'A thousand times better than her dad, anyway. And I knew the combination of Boscombe, Burton Bradstock and Poole rung a bell. The crimes all happened near places where we've foiled you in the past. I expect you've got hideaways in each.'

'I had no idea about this,' said Peter. 'It's all most impressive, Julian.'

'You can shut up,' said Julian. 'Don't think I've finished with you, either.'

'Well, this is a delightful surprise,' said Rupert. 'And Dick, Anne and George – Timmy, too! Lovely to see you, one last time. You all look so *well*.'

'Woof!' said Timmy, disapprovingly.

'As I say, nice to set eyes on you all. Family reunion and whatnot. But I think that's my helicopter ...'

The others all looked up into the evening sky. There was a rhythmic thumping noise coming out of the far distance, above the lapping of the waves.

'It'll be bringing my money,' said Rupert. 'Dorset

MINE! ALL MINE!

County Council paid up, after all. They had to. This is my last one. Five million quid will see me through, I think, and then maybe Anastasia will have me back too. She likes a winner.'

The thumping grew closer, and a dark shape loomed out

'What is the last member of the Secret Seven called?' Julian asked. 'I never can remember. Is it Wolfgang?'

of the sky. Rupert waved towards it, then smiled round at the others.

'You're all so sweet,' he said. He had to speak up, now. 'You don't understand that selfless heroes are totally old fashioned. They always were a joke, a fantasy to distract the simple-minded, while real people like me got things done and made money. Look at the world! Haven't you seen who's in charge? The way things have turned? Villains aren't villains anymore. They are the heroes, now! We've won! We took over while you were pickling things and making sourdough, and carefully recycling your plastic bags! Stop –' he splish-splashed the water with his shoe – 'kicking against the tide.'

Anne looked at the thick growth of silver beard, and the astrakhan coat (probably five thousand pounds' worth, and utterly inappropriate for living in the wild), ripped and stained all over. Looking at his bloodshot eyes it was hard to remember their always impeccable, always charming cousin, who never had a hair out of place, and had tricked them so many times before.

'You don't look like a winner,' said George. 'You look like a desperate tramp who's out on a limb. And who's doing something truly despicable to save his own guts.'

'I've *got* guts, though, George. I always liked you best, I have to admit.'

The helicopter came closer, and a bright cone of light swept the shore to try and locate them.

Rupert waved both hands over his head to attract attention.

'Rupert,' said Dick, 'I'm sorry, mate, but I don't think that's your money.'

'What else could it be?' shouted Rupert, angered by the note of sympathy in Dick's voice. He looked upwards, blinking in the white searchlight.

'An ambulance I called ten minutes ago,' said Anne.

'What's that?' Rupert yelled over the sound of the rotors.

'That's our NHS!' shouted everyone else.

All of a sudden, there was screaming everywhere. At least, that's how it seemed to Rupert. There was a crowd of people on the cliffs above (this was Janet, Barbara, Jack and the other members of the Secret Seven), shouting and clapping. Dick and Anne and George on the beach – and Julian and Peter too. None of them was concentrating on Rupert, or afraid of his gun. Instead, they were all cheering, waving and whooping into the sky. Rupert (who had literally been living in a cave) was disorientated.

He stepped backwards and tripped over something metallic. Pain clamped around his ankle and he fell to his knees. He waved frantically with both arms over his head. He tried to keep walking further out to sea, but pain grasped needily at his leg.

God, if only he could stop them all bloody yelling and clapping like that! He waved the gun around, but no one noticed.

And then he saw it, nuzzling at a bit of seaweed not ten feet away, next to that bloody metal contraption he'd just tripped over. That damned *bunny*. How it had tormented him! Eluding capture over and over, night after hungry night, while he was in the castle dungeon and could only make scavenging forays into the open air during the hours of darkness!

Now, seeing it so close, so plump and healthy, and apparently careless, Rupert could not help himself.

Feeling the dripping gun in his hand, he held the pistol level with the bunny's back, and squeezed the trigger.

CHAPTER THIRTEEN

Love Island

The helicopter had no problem finding where to land after the immense explosion that illuminated one side of the island.

The crater on the beach immediately started to fill with water, but the light showed a flat stretch of ground not far away. Soon, there were other vehicles on their way, too.

Cousin Rupert was not, as the Kirrins had first thought, blown to smithereens by the explosion of the old Second World War mine. He had been picked up and thrown about thirty feet by the blast, and had broken his leg nastily and taken a few pieces of shrapnel to the head. But he was still loudly, angrily and bloodily alive.

'That hardy git,' Julian said when the paramedics told him. 'I'll have to break it to the others. Bleeding ruddy hearts that they are, they'll probably be happy.'

Anne, meanwhile, had coaxed the helicopter pilot out

for a cup of tea, while maintaining a full two-metre distance at all times. It turned out that, although he was
piloting this air ambulance, he was also a police officer,
come to arrest Rupert Kirrin.

'You lads did me a right favour there, I reckon,' he
said, looking towards the crater. George beamed at being
included as one of the 'lads'. 'God knows what he would
have done when he realized the suitcase I'd brought along
for him only had old phone books in it. He was a loony,
thinking Dorset Council could get their hands on five mill,
just like that.'

'Considering his state of mind,' said George, 'he probably would have tried to make you fly him to Acapulco
at gunpoint.'

'Hmm,' said the police pilot. 'If he'd wanted Aber-
ystwyth, he might have had a better chance. I would say
there's a policy: "Dorset County Council doesn't negotiate
with terrorists." But I don't think it's ever come up before.'

'I'm glad this is all over,' said Julian. 'Three weeks
was quite enough. I thought I was going mad, at times.
But we pulled through! Any chance of a lift? I wonder if
the trains are still running.'

The others looked at him.

'Lockdown hasn't finished just because we've caught Rupert,' said Anne. 'It's still on. It might just be getting going!'

'Could be another three months, they're saying,' said the pilot. 'Those other seven youngsters were right to take that boat and clear out, I reckon.'

'Right,' said Julian. 'Three months. Right. Okay.' He took deep breaths for a few moments while the others looked on, amused. Then, suddenly, he snapped out of it.

'Now I think of it,' he said, 'a favour for a favour. Seeing as we rescued fifty million rolls of loo paper, can we have a dozen rolls to replenish our own stock? We've had no paper on this island that isn't in the covers of a book, for weeks.'

The pilot took this entirely seriously. 'You do that,' he said. 'I was in lockdown in Basra for weeks during one of my tours in Iraq. Terrifying. Was I ever glad I'd brought with me a copy of *The Way We Live Now*. Anthony Trollope's my favourite author but during those weeks, he and I,' the policeman said darkly, 'we came to an arrangement. You fetch those supplies, son. It's the very least we can do.'

'You *are* sweet,' said Anne, as Julian scurried off to the

'Lockdown could go on for another three months,' said Anne.
'Okay. Three months,' said Julian. 'Breathe. Just breathe.'

cave to take the Kirrins' share. 'And, now I think of it, could you please check on my aunt and uncle? They're in Kirrin Cottage, near Kirrin village, on the mainland, and are in *literal* lockdown. I mean, he's a high-level top-secret scientist, and decidedly odd to boot, and they're trapped inside the cottage by one of his contraptions. If you could make sure the authorities know, and check on them, maybe bring them food . . .'

'To Kirrin Cottage?' said the policeman. 'I know it. It'll be a pleasure to check on them, seeing as you asked me so nicely, and because you make a darn good cup of tea.'

'And make sure you tell them that we love them, very much?' said Anne. 'You *are* a darling . . .'

The morning was, once again, beautiful. With flagrant disregard for the odds, Britain was being graced with a spring and early summer of continuous cheerful sunshine.

'That raised bed is finished,' said Julian, resting on his spade. 'I think I've broken my back in three places, but it was worth it.'

'Well done, sweetie,' said Anne, giving him a decorous peck on the cheek. 'And Dick's got that barbecue up and running, more or less. You've really made this area start to look like a kitchen garden, as it might have been five hundred years ago!'

'And look,' said Dick, 'my Neil-yoghurt sourdough starter really yielded some goods. I think our first batch of sourdough flatbreads might be ready for lunch!'

Julian accepted the cup of tea Anne handed him, and, in trying to wipe a ticklish speck of dust from his nose, made a muddy smear across his right cheek. Then, trying to remove the speck a second time, he splashed hot tea on his toes.

'Much as it annoys me to admit it,' Julian said, 'it seems as though in this circumstance the right way really *was* just to keep calm and carry on. Anne, could you be a good egg and look up the Secret Seven again please,' said Julian. 'I'm always at a loss when we meet face to face, that there are, like, three of them whose names I don't know. I'm determined to remember this time.'

'Me too,' said Dick. 'I know there's a Janet and a Peter, and a Barbara . . .'

'Okay,' said Anne, typing on her phone. 'It says . . . "Did you mean Secret Seven, the pop-up restaurant on Bethnal Green Road?" No. "Did you mean Secret Seven, the upcoming comic-book adaptation starring Vin Diesel?"

No. Oh, listen to this: "Diesel plays a deadbeat Hawaiian ventriloquist who discovers he is the latest incarnation of an eternal superbeing, called—"'

'Sounds about his usual standard,' said Julian. 'Next!'

'"Did you mean Secret Seven, the highly prized secret recipe of herbs and spices that go into the batter at the eleven-location South Carolina restaurant chain Big Bubba's Bar-B-Q Pit?" No! Oh, wait, here we are. Yes. "English crime-fighting force"!'

'I knew they couldn't resist having a Wikipedia entry!' said Julian. 'So, come on, what *are* their names?'

'Peter, Janet, Barbara, Jack, Pam, Colin . . .' said Anne. She looked up. 'And? Anyone want to guess?'

'Roger?' asked Dick. 'Nigel? Derek?'

'Wolfgang?' said Julian. 'Mephistopheles? Xiùyīng?'

'No,' she said. 'George. They've also got a George!'

They all looked at their beloved cousin, who was sitting by the fire, engrossed in her task of wrangling some blackened tins with an old-fashioned tin opener.

'You know,' George said, perplexed, 'I'm not sure this *is* bully beef.' She had four pots open on the little table by her side, and she was sniffing them suspiciously, one after the other. 'I'd almost swear it's a sort of preserved

103

vegetable. Cabbage, maybe. I'd almost be ready to swear it was . . . sauerkraut?'

Anne picked up one of the cans, poked a fork in and took a taste.

'Hmm,' she said. 'Doesn't go off, sauerkraut.'

'Great for gut health,' said Julian.

'And those bottles of gin did turn out to be schnapps, after all,' said Dick, swilling some in a glass. 'So, does that seem to suggest that . . . our friend in the bunker by the shore . . .'

'. . . whose radio Rupert used, and whose booze he drank . . .' muttered George.

Dick swallowed his schnapps. Julian took a tentative slurp of tea. George picked her nose. Timmy sniffed in one of the cans, and then retreated, sneezing.

'Well,' said Anne, 'I wonder what people made of the Secret Seven turning up with a load of face masks decorated all over with swastikas. We never got a clear look at the material, after all, because we were always working in the evening, and by firelight!'

'On-brand for those guys, if you ask me,' said Julian. 'Serves them bloody right for nicking it.'

'And we got credit for recovering all those crucial supplies,' said Anne. 'Really, thanks to pure chance.'

'Thanks to Julian's pure unadulterated fury,' said Dick. 'Which was fun to watch.'

'I regret nothing,' said Julian. 'That man pushed me too far. He did so deliberately. Even the police helicopter pilot agreed.'

'Woof!' said Timmy, as everyone gathered round the barbecue.

Between the fronds of grass, Timmy glimpsed a shape that had been tormenting him for weeks. The sleek fur. The nose twitch. The meek, doubtful (and yet somehow deeply calculating and evil) nibble.

'Woof!' said Timmy, leaping out to chase after him. 'Woof! Woof!'